Dedications

In loving memory of my grandparents Edward & Annie Wong
and my wonderful father Gerald Takamatsu.
~T.P.

To my sister, Christine Robinson.
~D.R.

ISLAND HERITAGE™
PUBLISHING
A DIVISION OF THE MADDEN CORPORATION

**94-411 Kōʻaki Street
Waipahu, Hawaiʻi 96797-2806
Orders: (800) 468-2800
Information: (808) 564-8800
Fax: (808) 564-8877
islandheritage.com**

**ISBN: 1-59700-758-7
First Edition, Twelfth Printing—2015
COP 140411**

TOO MANY
MANGOS
A Story About Sharing
Written by **Tammy Paikai** • Illustrated by **Don Robinson**

ISLAND HERITAGE™
PUBLISHING

Kama and his sister, Nani, love to climb the giant mango tree when they visit their grandpa's house. Kama can climb up high. He helps Nani find a special branch to sit on.

Grandpa comes outside and asks Kama to pick some mangos.
Kama reaches and tugs on the mangos one by one and
passes them to Nani, and she passes them to Grandpa.
There are big ones, small ones, ripe ones, green ones,
and some have brown spots on them.

Grandpa looks over the huge pile of mangos. He says, "There are too many mangos for our little family. Take some down the road and share them with our neighbors."

Kama and Nani load the mangos in a little red wagon
and pull it down the road to the first house.

"Aloha, Aunty Pua! Grandpa said to give some mangos to you," Nani exclaims.
"Mahalo children. These mangos will make delicious mango bread," says
Aunty Pua. "These spotty ones are perfect!"

"Here are some banana macadamia nut muffins that I baked this morning. Mahalo for sharing!" says Aunty Pua.

12

They see their friends at the next house.
Kama and Nani sing out, "Aloooha, Momi
and Kawai. Grandpa has too many mangos."
"Oooh, I love to eat fresh ripe mangos," says
Momi. They both take a few golden yellow
ones and say, "Mahalo for the mangos.
Here are some papayas for your family."

Kama and Nani visit the next neighbor. "Aloha , Mr. Wong. Grandpa has some mangos for you today," Kama says. He takes a few green mangos and says, "Green mango with shoyu, vinegar, and chili pepper water is the best! Mrs. Wong made some guava jam. Here is a jar for you."

Each neighbor that they visit gives them something in return. Lani likes pickled mango. She takes the half-ripe mangos and gives Kama some bananas.

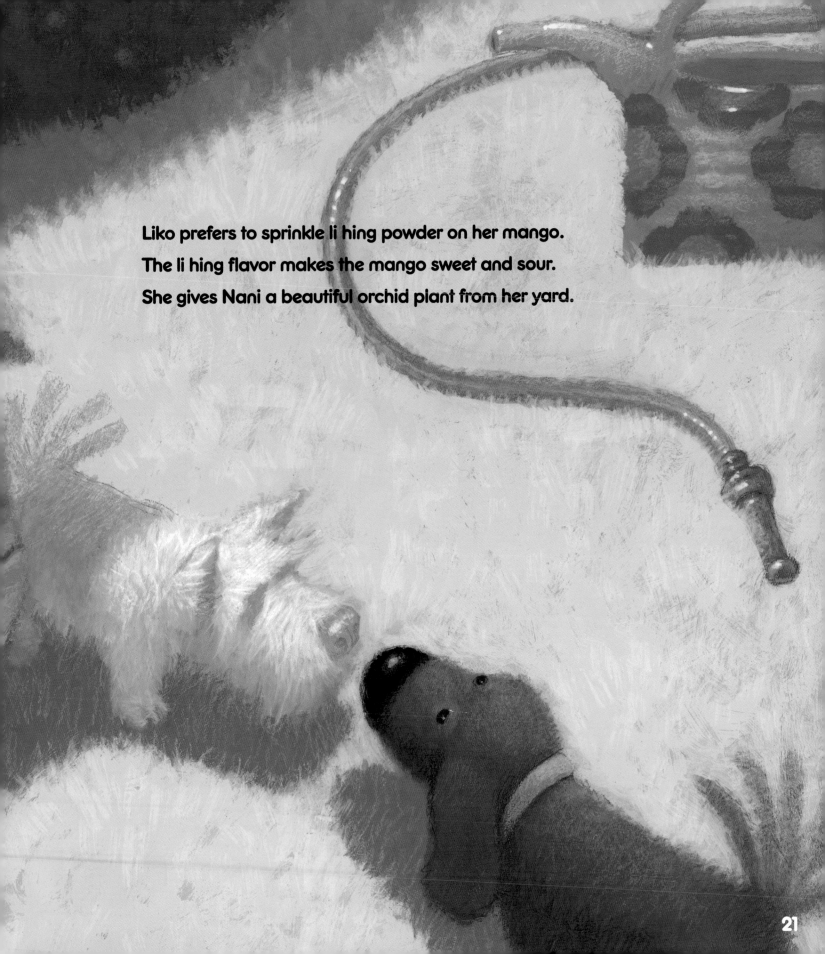

Liko prefers to sprinkle li hing powder on her mango.

The li hing flavor makes the mango sweet and sour.

She gives Nani a beautiful orchid plant from her yard.

They finally went to every house on the block and realized that although the mangos were gone, their wagon was completely full.

Grandpa sees Kama and Nani returning home. Nani excitedly tells Grandpa, "We were able to share all of our mangos!" Kama shows Grandpa all of their mahalo gifts from the neighbors.

Nani puts the orchid plant on the table,
Kama gives each of them a muffin with
guava jam on it, and Grandpa combines
the bananas, papayas, and mangos
together to make a fresh fruit salad.
Nani picks up a big slice of mango.
She smiles and says, "We're lucky
Grandpa had too many mangos!"

The End